Look at Us

HOUGHTON MIFFLIN   BOSTON

Printed in The United States Of America

ISBN-13: 978-0-547-07439-9
ISBN-10: 0-547-07439-5

56789-0868-15 14 13 12 11 10
4500227284

Contents

All In

by Bonnie Whitmark

Can you see Kit?
Kit has fun in a bag.

Do you see pups?

Pups can tug, tug, tug, tug.

Pups can run down.

Pups can run, run, run, run.

Big dogs can dig.

Big dogs dug, dug, dug, dug.

Big dogs can run down.
Big dogs can run, run, run.

This big cat can run.
It can go up, up, up.

Bug and Cat

by James Parsons
illustrated by John Hovell

Bug and Cat can play.
Fun, fun, fun, fun!

Bug can hop up and down.
Up, up, up. Fun, fun, fun!

Cat can hit this for fun.
Rum, tum, tum! Rum, tum!

Bug can hum. Cat can hum.
Hum, Bug. Hum, Cat.

Bug can sit on a rug.
Cat can sit on a rug.

Do Bug and Cat run?
Bug and Cat run, run, run!

Win a Cup!

by Todd Turriro

illustrated by Marilyn Janovitz

Meg can run, run, run!
Meg can win a big cup.

13

Ken can hit and run.
Ken can win a big cup.

Pam can hit ten down.
Pam can win a big cup.

Wes can help Lon.

Lon can help Wes.

Wes can win a big cup!
Lon can win a big cup!

We have a cup.

Wes Can Help

by Anne Miranda
illustrated by Susan Lexa

Len and Lin get on a big jet.
Len and Lin can have fun.

Wes led Len. Len can sit.
Wes led Lin. Lin can sit.

Len let Wes help him.

Wes got the big bag up.

Wes got Len a hot dog.

Wes got Lin a sub.

The big jet is down.

Len can run. Lin can run.

Len had fun. Lin had fun.
Wes had fun.

Vet on a Job!

by Anne Miranda

Ed the vet can look at Max.

Sal the vet can look at Viv.
Sal fed the cub.

Val the vet can look at Vin.

Vin can run now.

Bev the vet can look at Zeb.
Zeb can not hop.

Vic the vet can look at Zig.
Zig can not zip out!

Lib the vet can look at Sam.
Lib can pat Sam.

Roz the Vet

by Terry Rengifo
illustrated by Joe Cepeda

Roz the vet can help a pet!
Roz can zip in a red van.

Roz can look at a pet pig.
Roz fed it. Gob, gob, gob.

Roz the vet can help a pet!
Roz can zip in a red van.

Vic had a bad cut.

Can Roz fix it? Roz can!

Tab Cat got out. Tab ran.
Tab had fun. Tab ran up.

Tab can look at Roz.

Roz will get Tab down.

Not Yet

by Nancy Spencer

Cat, do not get up yet!
Nap on the red cat mat.

Dog, do not get up yet!
Nap on the big rug.

Hen, do not get up yet!
Nap in the hen box.

Pig, do not get up yet!
Nap in the pig pen.

Fox, do not get up yet!
Nap in the fox den.

Bat, get up! Bat, take off!
Bats can quit at sun up!

Can Not Quit Yet

by Antonio Winkler
illustrated by Rick Brown

Yes, yes! Ben can hit it.
Ben hit the tub, rum tum!

Rum! Tum! Tum!
Ben can not quit yet.

Yes, yes! Kim can dig.
Kim can dig, dig, dig.

Kim can dig, dig, dig.
Kim can not quit yet.

Yes, yes! It can take off.
Zip, zip, Meg! Zip, zip!

It can zip, zip, zip.
Meg can not quit yet.

Max Is Down

by Sam Bateman

illustrated by John Wallner

Max can go up, up, up.
Max will go up, up, up.

Max is up, up, up.

Max can not get down.

"Help!" said Max.

Bud ran.

Can Bud get Max down?

Look! Bud can not get Max.

Tom ran. Can Tom get Max?
Look! Tom can not get Max.
Big Zeb can help us.

Big Zeb can tug, tug, tug.

Will Max get down?

Tug, Big Zeb, tug!

Will Max get down?

Yes. He did!

Big Zeb got Max down.

A Fun Job

by Priscilla Banab

illustrated by Jeff Mack

Ted has a job.

Deb has a job.

"Find nuts," said Mom.
"Get nuts. Get lots."
Ted runs. Deb runs.

Ted got nuts. Deb got nuts.
It is a fun job to get nuts.
It is fun, fun, fun.

Ted hid nuts.

Ted hid nuts in pots.

Deb hid nuts in pots.

Look at the pots.

Can Ted and Deb see nuts?

No, Ted and Deb can not.

Ted hid nuts in pots.

Deb hid nuts in pots.

What is in the pots now?

Word Lists

All In

Decodable Words
Target Skill: *Words with u*
dug, fun, pups, run, tug, up

Words Using Previously Taught Skills
bag, big, can, cat, dig, dogs, has, in, it, Kit

High-Frequency Words
New
do, down

Previously Taught
a, go, see, this, you

Bug and Cat

Decodable Words
Target Skill: *Words with u*
bug, fun, hum, rug, rum, run, tum, up

Words Using Previously Taught Skills
can, cat, hit, hop, on, sit

High-Frequency Words
New
do, down

Previously Taught
a, and, I, is, me, my, the, a, and, for, play, this

Win a Cup!

page 13

Decodable Words
Target Skill: *Words with l, w*
Lon, Wes, win

Words Using Previously Taught Skills
big, can, cup, hit, Ken, Meg, Pam,
run, ten

High-Frequency Words
New
have, help

Previously Taught
a, and, down, we

Wes Can Help

page 19

Decodable Words
Target Skill: *Words with l, w*
led, Len, let, Lin, Wes

Words Using Previously Taught Skills
bag, big, can, dog, fun, get, got,
him, hot, is, jet, on, run, sit, sub

High-Frequency Words
New
have, help

Previously Taught
a, and, down, the

Vet on a Job!

page 25

Decodable Words

Target Skill: *Words with v, z*
Bev, Val, vet, Vic, Vin, Viv, Zeb, Zig, zip

Words Using Previously Taught Skills
at, can, cub, Ed, fed, hop, Lib, Max, not, pat, run, Sal, Sam

High-Frequency Words
New
look, out

Previously Taught
the, now

Roz the Vet

page 31

Decodable Words

Target Skill: *Words with v, z*
Roz, van, vet, Vic, zip

Words Using Previously Taught Skills
at, bad, can, Cat, cut, fed, fix, fun, get, gob, got, had, in, it, pet, pig, ran, red, Tab, up

High-Frequency Words
New
look, out

Previously Taught
a, down, help, the, will

63

Not Yet

page 37

Decodable Words
Target Skill: *Words with y, q*
quit, yet

Words Using Previously Taught Skills
at, bat, bats, bet, big, box, can,
cat, den, dog, fox, get, hen, in,
mat, nap, not, on, pen, pig, red,
sun, up

High-Frequency Words
New
off, take

Previously Taught
do, the

Can Not Quit Yet

page 43

Decodable Words
Target Skill: *Words with y, q*
quit, yes, yet

Words Using Previously Taught Skills
Ben, can, dig, hit, it, Kim, Meg,
not, rum, tub, tum, zip

High-Frequency Words
New
off, take

Previously Taught
the

Max Is Down

page 49

Decodable Words
Target Skill: *Words with a, e, i, o, u*
big, Bud, can, did, get, got, is, Max,
not, ran, Tom, tug, up, us, Zeb

High-Frequency Words
down, go, help, look, said,
will

A Fun Job

page 55

Decodable Words
Target Skill: *Words with a, e, i, o, u*
can, Deb, fun, get, got, has, hid, in,
is, it, job, lots, Mom, pots, not, nuts,
runs, Ted

High-Frequency Words
a, and, at, find, look, no,
said, see, the, to, now,
what